so go the ghosts of méxico,

part one

Matthew Paul Olmos

A Samuel French Acting Edition

SAMUEL FRENCH

FOUNDED 1830

SAMUELFRENCH.COM
SAMUELFRENCH-LONDON.CO.UK

FOR PRODUCTION ENQUIRIES

UNITED STATES AND CANADA
Info@SamuelFrench.com
1-866-598-8449

UNITED KINGDOM AND EUROPE
Plays@SamuelFrench-London.co.uk
020-7255-4302

Each title is subject to availability from Samuel French, depending upon country of performance. Please be aware that SO GO THE GHOSTS OF MÉXICO may not be licensed by Samuel French in your territory. Professional and amateur producers should contact the nearest Samuel French office or licensing partner to verify availability.

MUSIC USE NOTE

Licensees are solely responsible for obtaining formal written permission from copyright owners to use copyrighted music in the performance of this play and are strongly cautioned to do so. If no such permission is obtained by the licensee, then the licensee must use only original music that the licensee owns and controls. Licensees are solely responsible and liable for all music clearances and shall indemnify the copyright owners of the play(s) and their licensing agent, Samuel French, against any costs, expenses, losses and liabilities arising from the use of music by licensees. Please contact the appropriate music licensing authority in your territory for the rights to any incidental music.

IMPORTANT BILLING AND CREDIT REQUIREMENTS

If you have obtained performance rights to this title, please refer to your licensing agreement for important billing and credit requirements.

SO GO THE GHOSTS OF MÉXICO, PART ONE was first produced by La MaMa e.t.c. in New York City on April 11, 2013 (Mia Yoo, Artistic Director; Beverly Petty, Producing Director). It was directed by Meiyin Wang, with set design by Nick Benacerraf, sound design by Elizabeth Rhodes, lighting design Jeanette Oi-Suk Yew, and costume design by Alice Tavener. The Stage Manager was Danielle Thomsen. The cast was as follows:

A BRAVE WOMAN IN MÉXICO	Laura Butler Rivera
THE POLICE CHIEF	Luis Moreno
THE HUSBAND	Bernardo Cubria
EL MORETE	José Joaquin Perez
GÜERO	Peter O'Connor

SO GO THE GHOSTS OF MÉXICO, PART ONE was developed in part by Rising Circle Collective and Duke University Department of Theatre, and with Teddy Cañez, Doug Darwin, Audrey Esparza, Flor De Liz Perez, Felix Solis, and José Zayas.

PART I

a brave woman in méxico

THE PEOPLE

A BRAVE WOMAN IN MÉXICO
THE POLICE CHIEF
THE HUSBAND
EL MORETE
GÜERO

SETTING

México, present day

THE BEGINNING

(An emptying dirt and gravel parking lot: vacant spaces and cars-recently-left surrounded by cars-abandoned-who-the-fuck-knows.)

*(**MARI** and **HUSBAND** fuck in an emptied car.)*

HUSBAND. Lemme just –

MARI. Yea, I know, it's –

HUSBAND. You're on my –

MARI. I know, I'm trying to –

HUSBAND. Will you get…over –

MARI. I don't want be…over, I wanna be right…on…this…

HUSBAND. Fine then lift your –

MARI. I can't, you go around –

HUSBAND. Mari, I can't keep it in if I can't –

MARI. You're a man, if there's a way to keep it in, you will.

> *(**HUSBAND** tries a different approach; they find a rhythm.)*

HUSBAND. See that. Lookit us –

MARI. Will you/just –

HUSBAND. See how we can be –

MARI. No words.

> *(Just as **HUSBAND** feels in sync, **MARI** pulls off. On their separation, we hear a breaking of static; they both notice, but think nothing of it.)*

HUSBAND. Okay…

MARI. This isn't –

HUSBAND. Wow. I know that look.

MARI. I'm not looking at you, I'm just –

HUSBAND. What? *(pause)* Say it.

MARI. Tomorrow.

HUSBAND. Tomorrow what.

MARI. I have to go, I do.

HUSBAND. How is that gonna work?

MARI. I'll show up and they'll have been expecting me to show up.

HUSBAND. I knew it. I knew you didn't tell them.

MARI. I told you I wasn't sure.

HUSBAND. No, you told me you had spoken to them and they understood.

(beat)

MARI. I tried to do this, you know. Here, with you. I... I just –

HUSBAND. You just what.

MARI. I just don't...believe in...you and me creating, what, some life –

HUSBAND. Some life???

MARI. That'll just, what, add to the –

HUSBAND. We can live our lives, or we can stop living our lives.

MARI. No, we can do something all this shit, or we can just...

HUSBAND. And how is not having a child –

MARI. I'm not saying no. I want what you do, Love, I do. But not like this...this isn't what I want our child to be born into.

HUSBAND. If you do this, there is no our child.

MARI. Thank you, for supporting me so –

HUSBAND. Supporting you?

MARI. Yes.

HUSBAND. The moment you walk into your police station tomorrow –

What I support is the mother of my daughter waking up every day. Alive.

(beat)

MARI. Well. I'm all wet, how're you?

> (**MARI** *pulls her clothes back up*)

HUSBAND. How does a *mother* actually go through with something like this.

MARI. Easy, she goes through it alone.

> *(Static enters; both feel the vibration; they look around.)*

HUSBAND. What is –

MARI. I dunno.

HUSBAND. It's like a –

MARI. Is the car on?

> (**HUSBAND** *checks the ignition, no key. He gets out and pops the hood.*)

Well?

> (**HUSBAND** *looks around, then gets back in the car.*)

HUSBAND. No engine.

> (**MARI** *reaches out to the radio, she turns the dial.*)

Mari, don't –

> *(Sounds of music burst from the static;* **MARI** *turns it up with wonder, as it is unlike anything she has ever heard.)*

Will you lower it, what if it's some sort of signal, or –

MARI. Es beautiful.

HUSBAND. It's not plugged into anything.

> (**HUSBAND** *turns the volume dial: nothing. He tries the station dial: nothing. It looks as though* **MARI** *is hearing something from so deep within her that she cannot help but grin in disbelief.* **HUSBAND** *looks out the window with concern. We watch and listen as the ins and outs of static and music weave throughout the car, illuminating a*

divide between **MARI** *and* **HUSBAND***, it looks as though an invisible wall is building between them.* **MARI** *grows illuminated, while* **HUSBAND** *fades. As this happens, the music begins to take over.*)

(**MARI** *begins to hum along.*)

(*The music jolts into alarming with a scratch which rumbles into the coarse sound of tires crushing onto gravel as a black SUV rolls up.*)

(**MARI** *and* **HUSBAND** *freeze as sounds of a car door opening and slamming make the music static. Exit from the driver door* **EL MORETE***, who looks about, trying to place the music. He pulls an automatic and begins looking in various cars*)

EL MORETE. *(to the lot)* So…whoever's like playing the music, can you at least change the station or some shit, cuz this song sounds like my sister's ass; it's loud and kinda repetitive.

(**MARI** *excitedly changes the station.*)

Uh, thank you. I guess. But like why don't you just shut off the music like altogether –

(**MARI** *turns it up.*)

Oh, okay, so es like that, huh? Es like that? Well you know what, I actually like this song, so you can turn that shit up to the fuckin'stars.

(**MARI** *turns it back to his sister's ass.* **EL MORETE** *points his gun at nobody.*)

Alright, who the fuck! Huh? Who the fuck is…who the fuck is playing that – ? C'mon, get your ass out here so I can…

(**MARI** *lowers the song.* **EL MORETE** *relaxes.*)

See, now we can like hear each other an' shit. I can actually like think.

(MARI plays sister's ass. EL MORETE shoots several rounds into wherever. EL MORETE's mobile immediately rings, he answers)

(into phone) Nobody! *(pause)* No, es not like that. Some *puto* is playing like this really fucking annoying song – *(pause)* Well, lower your window then, es like a fuckin'outdoor concert out here an' shit –

(The back SUV window lowers. A moment. It raises.)

(into phone) How the fuck can you *like* this song, this song's – *(pause)* No, es not just a car radio, this shit is like...all around or something. *(pause)* Look, I am telling you, there is somebody in this lot playin'music what I don't like, like on fucking purpose. *(pause) Sí. Sí. Yo entiendo.*

(EL MORETE obediently moves back to the car. MARI turns sister's ass loud. EL MORETE ignites, firing off several rounds before the back car door opens again, EL MORETE obediently gets back into the SUV and drives off.)

(MARI sits staring at the car radio, moving the volume up and down, flicking with the station.)

HUSBAND. What're you smiling for.

MARI. I don't know/I –

HUSBAND. No, really. Explain it to me. Your face.

MARI. Stoppit.

HUSBAND. Well, I'm sure your daughter will sleep just absolutely sound tonight, every night, with what you just did to us.

(The car gives way to the bedroom, daylight to darkness. HUSBAND falls to sleep, MARI stays standing, as the darkness turns to morning. Time is fast. MARI gets ready for work; a bulletproof vest to her body. MARI hums along to the music, which now flavors their home. HUSBAND's breathing

sounds like static as he sleeps; occasionally bumping up as he tosses and turns. **MARI** *looks down at* **HUSBAND,** *and rhythmically moves out from their home to the Outside. When she opens the front door, she is met with a flurry of beautiful sounds. She walks into it, closing the door behind her. With this* **HUSBAND** *sits up, we hear static attack him as he looks to see the other half of his marriage bed empty. He gets up hurriedly, moving to the front door, however when he opens the door, he is met with a barrage of static which filters into the sounds of a car pulling off.* **HUSBAND** *watches it go, then returns into the home. He looks about strangely as the mix of music and static fill the home. He tries to pinpoint a source, but cannot find one. He kneels, begins talking to somebody younger.)*

(to **MIJA***)* Hey there, Mija. No es okay, don't get up. I'm just awake to see you *Mamá* off to work, huh. *(pause)* Wha's that? *(pause)* Oh, don't you worry, Mija, she'll be back tonight. *(pause)* Awh, Mija, I know, I know. I wish she didn't have to go too. *(pause)* No, she'll be gone all – *(pause)* Uh huh. Yea, Mija, me too. But hey, I'll tell you what, when you get up in a few hours, why don't you get yourself ready something pretty, huh? Brush yer teeth real good, put a comb all the way through an' then maybe you an' me take a ride into town, huh? Hey, who knows, maybe we'll even see –

*(***HUSBAND** *hugs invisible daughter tight. He holds her as though he is afraid she is not real. Lights dim on father and daughter surrounded by the mix of static and music;* **HUSBAND** *looks around unsure where it is all coming from.)*

Scene Two

> (**MARI** *stands nervously in an empty police station. She smiles and fidgets as if an entire room is staring at her.*)

MARI. *Buenos días. Soy Mari.*

> (*Awkward pause.* **MARI** *pulls a plastic tub from her desk area.*)

Pongan sus pistolas en el recipiente, por favor.

> (**MARI** *lifts the lid of the tub and deposits a revolver inside. She holds the tub out for others. She waits.*)

Pongan sus pistolas, por favor.

> (*She waits. Sound of static responding to her.*)

Porque no vamos a perseguir a ningún cartel en la ciudad.

> (*She goes to the wall which has a put'together map of photographs of cartel bosses, lieutenants, soldiers, of cartel members, and a map showing cartel territories and pathways. She begins removing all such items, and places them into a file cabinet.*)

Ninguno.

> (*She holds out the tub again. Several bursts of static.* **MARI** *lets down the tub. She tries a different approach.*)

Lo primero que vamos a hacer es ir de puerta en puerta y hablar en persona con todos los papás y mamás que todavía vivan aquí. Para asegurarnos que mantengan a sus hijos cerca, que todos los niños de la ciudad vayan a la escuela. No podemos permitir que el dinero de los carteles atraiga a ningún niño. ¿Entienden? Por favor. ¿Entienden?

> (*Several new notes of music sound and give way to the sound of revolvers being placed in the tub.* **MARI** *thanks each as they place their weapons inside. She then closes the lid.*)

Gracias.

(The room empties, **MARI** *pulls the car radio and turns up the sound. She looks up as if everybody looked back at her strangely.)*

MARI. *Es sólo música, mientras trabajamos.*

*(***MARI***'s eyes are lit by the computer screen, she smiles as she types. A few moments, she then begins to fill out reports then hand them to clerks who are not there, assign equipment then hand off to officers who cannot be seen. Music builds as she does this, she finds her rhythm. A few moments of progress and music. Time moves fast. Enter* **HUSBAND***, he watches her work a few moments before she notices. He picks up the car radio)*

HUSBAND. Just a car radio, huh.

MARI. It's nice to see you too.

HUSBAND. For all you know that could be some –

MARI. It's not a secret. Where I am. What I'm doing.

*(***HUSBAND*** puts down radio. Beat.)*

HUSBAND. So?

MARI. What.

HUSBAND. How was it? Your first day.

MARI. I think they're waiting to see how they feel about me.

HUSBAND. How *they* feel about you.

MARI. Yes. They.

*(Beat. ***HUSBAND*** makes to kneel.)*

Do Not Do That Here.

HUSBAND. She asked.

MARI. I'm at work.

HUSBAND. "What's that, Mija, last night you couldn't sleep?"

MARI. She slept fine, what're you –

HUSBAND. "Awh, Mija, do you know what all that was? That was just car backfiring. Do you know what car'backfiring is?"

MARI. Please.

HUSBAND. Do you?

MARI. What do you talk to her like that for, she has ears, she has eyes.

HUSBAND. It's just from a car, Mija. It's just car noises an' that's all. Y'see, Mija, sometimes there's this tiny explosion in the engine of a car; you know what an engine is, right? *(pause)* You're so smart. Kiss?

> *(He waits for a kiss, but gets none.)*

So, sometimes, Mija, not always, just sometimes there's an explosion in the wrong room of the engine and it goes off like boom."

MARI. *(to MIJA)* "You know, Mija, boom like when we hear the guns go off. That's the kinda boom your father means."

HUSBAND. "Car backfiring happens cuz a few reasons, Mija, but mostly it's prolly just that the little doors inside the little car engine weren't shut properly. And so the car jumps like that! In fact, sometimes in a car backfire you even see a little flame come out the back of the car pushing it forward, more forward than the driver meant the car to go."

MARI. She knows what you're doing, it won't work forever, what you're doing.

HUSBAND. "Your *Mamá* might not be home tonight after all. But don't worry, Mija, if she's not, you can sleep in our –"

MARI. You're getting worse. You know that, right?

HUSBAND. And you, you're not even pregnant yet, but you're already the worst mother I can even imagine.

> *(Music suffers. A few moments. MARI and HUSBAND both notice.)*

MARI. You talk like that. You do. On good days, you speak to me so sweetly that all I want is to make everything you want to come to true. But on your bad days, you take our daughter's tongue, you use it against me, you look at me, you speak at me like that. You do.

HUSBAND. Well, when there's no ways left to reach someone, what else can we do.

MARI. What is it you even want our daughter for, huh? Is she something you believe will make the world better than it is, or do you just want one?

HUSBAND. ...is...is that all what you think of her? Just...

(As **MARI** begins to speak, the music strengthens.)

MARI. I believe that what I'm doing is the most mother anybody could be. Because it's not just for the beautiful what would be our child, Love. This is for her children, for theirs after. For the tens of thousands of parents and children buried or waiting to be buried in this what we call country.

HUSBAND. Your speechwriting...it's showing signs of improvement.

(Music reaches.)

MARI. Los Zetas, Juárez, Sinaloa. Los Narcos will be the only family still living left. And what do you think our daughter-to-be would have to do for money in a family like that? (pause) So you can plan your little family, Love, but today, right now, before our daughter is even conceived, I am creating for her the most choices she will ever have in life. And so we can do like you do, and care only what's in our bedrooms, or we can try harder for another kind of world for her to be born into.
But you'll never –
Y'know what, go. And don't come back. Not here, not again. I don't want you, nor her, through those doors where I'm trying to do something.

HUSBAND. Why don't you tell her yourself. Or can you not even bring yourself to talk to her anymore?

MARI. I believe in our daughter more than you can even understand, Love. Now go, I'll see you at home.

> (**MARI** *shows* **HUSBAND** *out; he exits; as he does the music swells; she takes it in. Time passes. White out.*)

Scene Three

(**MARI** *walks from station to home amidst a rolling of music. She amazes in all directions.*)

(*She enters her home;* **HUSBAND** *sleeps. She looks at him, pets his head. She shares a moment with him before hearing a sound; as though when somebody is on the premises.* **HUSBAND** *shoots up.*)

HUSBAND. What was –

MARI. Shh, I heard it too.

(*Another noise.* **HUSBAND** *gets out of bed. Both fright as the front door swings open*)

Who's – who's there – what d'you want –

(**HUSBAND** *holds a lamp up in defense. Enter* **DEAD POLICE CHIEF**, *a ravaged body more than a person, still wearing a tattered, bloodied uniform*)

Stop, Do Not Move.

DEAD POLICE CHIEF. …SHHHH…

(**DEAD POLICE CHIEF** *listens for the music. He finds it.*)

Oh, there she is.

(**DEAD POLICE CHIEF** *begins searching the room for a source.*)

HUSBAND. What're you –

DEAD POLICE CHIEF. Aht aht aht.

(**DEAD POLICE CHIEF** *motions silence.* **MARI** *stares, she moves closer.*)

MARI. (*to* **DEAD POLICE CHIEF**) Are you…

HUSBAND. What.

DEAD POLICE CHIEF. Where is it?

HUSBAND. (*to* **DEAD POLICE CHIEF**) Where is what?

MARI. (*to* **DEAD POLICE CHIEF**) You're the –

DEAD POLICE CHIEF. Where is it coming from, *Señora Policía?*

MARI. How did you –

DEAD POLICE CHIEF. *(to MARI)* Ma'ri…

HUSBAND. How does he know your –

DEAD POLICE CHIEF. *(to HUSBAND)* I ain't goin'tell you again, husband'man.

MARI. …I know you…

DEAD POLICE CHIEF. *La música,* where is it?

MARI. I… I don't know.

DEAD POLICE CHIEF. No? Well tha's too bad then.

> *(DEAD POLICE CHIEF walks at HUSBAND, stripping the lamp from him and putting his hand to HUSBAND's throat.)*

MARI. stop, freeze…

DEAD POLICE CHIEF. Now, you point me in the direction of *la música, Señora Policía,* or…

MARI. Look, I don't know, I don't know where or what it is, it just is!

DEAD POLICE CHIEF. When did it start?

MARI. Let him up!

DEAD POLICE CHIEF. …

MARI. A couple days ago.

> *(HUSBAND tries to mumble.)*

DEAD POLICE CHIEF. I ain't goin'tell you again, choking' man, SHHH. This *policía* talk.

MARI. What do you want, please, he can't –

DEAD POLICE CHIEF. WHERE IS IT!?

MARI. I DON'T KNOW, IT JUST PLAYS, NOW LET HIM UP, YOU WEAK FUCKING GHOSTS!!!!!

> *(DEAD POLICE CHIEF steps back at her weight; releases HUSBAND who falls to the floor, MARI goes to him. DEAD POLICE CHIEF looks down at HUSBAND.)*

DEAD POLICE CHIEF. *(to* **HUSBAND***)* What kinda man don't know how to protect his house.

MARI. You grabbed him.

DEAD POLICE CHIEF. *(to* **HUSBAND***)* Me, I didn't even know I *could* grab him. But then I seen his eyes, and they told me that I could.

MARI. Leave him alone.

DEAD POLICE CHIEF. *(to* **HUSBAND***)* What kinda man lets his wife talk for him like that for?

       *(***DEAD POLICE CHIEF** *looks at his hands, his grip)*

Lookit these…they were never any good for me before, but now…

HUSBAND. What kinda police puts his hands on innocent –

DEAD POLICE CHIEF. The kind of police that is…your wife's predecessor.

HUSBAND. …what're you talkin – ?

MARI. What do you want.

HUSBAND. But you were shot.

DEAD POLICE CHIEF. Shot?

    (to **MARI***)* Is that what you told to him, your husband? That I was "shot"?

HUSBAND. Hey, get away from her. Do you hear me?

      *(***HUSBAND** *tries to get between* **MARI** *and* **DEAD POLICE CHIEF.***)*

DEAD POLICE CHIEF. What's a matter, Mari, you don't tell to your husband everything?

HUSBAND. Tell to me what everything? *(pause)* Hey. Tell to me what? *(pause)* Hey!

DEAD POLICE CHIEF. *(to* **MARI***)* Would you like to tell him, or should I?

MARI. …

DEAD POLICE CHIEF. *(to* **HUSBAND***)* It's a shame you don't read the papers, non'readingman.

HUSBAND. I read the papers, just not the –

DEAD POLICE CHIEF. Well. Never thought of my life as a detail. But

> (**DEAD POLICE CHIEF** *removes his head*)

since you an' your wife don't like to talk…

HUSBAND. …holyshit…

> (*Beat. Darkness flows into the room.* **DEAD POLICE CHIEF** *listens to it.*)

DEAD POLICE CHIEF. Do you hear that? *That's* what it sound like when their breaths on the back of my neck while they yanked my arms behind to put the blindfold. And I could hear while they do the same to my officers.

Under the motor of that, I can hear my throat coughing on the mucus and tears in my mouth mixed with the blood. I try to hear myself talk, but my mouth don't wanna talk.

Then I hear the tires riding us just off the highway, the click of the car back opening up. And then the sounds of my knee'bones go crack as they empty us out the car and onto the dust. Ain't that some shit? I think, even if I make it out this somehow, I'll have fucked up knees. Just like everybody else who live too long.

Then the shots, one by one. Screaming. Body parts going gone. An' I don't know what about how your life sound, still'breathing man, but I couldn't quite place the sound of my own head banging around the inside of that ice chest. Thumping. Bouncing. Sometimes a soft spot and it go squish.

Then afterwards, I hear only darkness. I guess they quieted the book on me.

> (*Music reaches,* **DEAD POLICE CHIEF** *gains strength,* **MARI** *moves closer to him, as though drawn.*)

But then, from all my quiet that was my new home, I hear…*la música*. Calling me to come close. And before I can even hear the sounds of my thoughts telling me how to make that happen… I hear the walk of my own boot heels, going up your door, *Policía*.

DEAD POLICE CHIEF. An' now, my question to you, Mari, is what did you call to me for?

MARI. ...I didn't call you.

DEAD POLICE CHIEF. Oh, but you did. And now lookit me, with *la música* pumping through me, I can do whatever it is you wish, I can walk back out there and put these hands on any motherfucker with a gun.

MARI. But you never, you never hurt anyone –

DEAD POLICE CHIEF. No. I tried to keep my distance from them, but...

HUSBAND. But what?

DEAD POLICE CHIEF. How do you protect anyone, if you're not allowed to protect them?

HUSBAND. You should be now with your family.

DEAD POLICE CHIEF. What family. You think I'm standing here meanwhile I got a family??

HUSBAND. Okay, but you must have/there must be some –

DEAD POLICE CHIEF. Somewhere more impressive to be? Well, me, was never married, no kids. And my guess: when you die, you can be *where*ver you wish to, *when*ever, *how*ever. But it has to have existed.

HUSBAND. Well, but, Señor, what about –

DEAD POLICE CHIEF. Heaven? Hell? In'between?

HUSBAND. Yes, of course.

DEAD POLICE CHIEF. Listen, cuz this shit is like first'hand. My guess: Heaven is being able to return to whatever happiness you held. As for Hell, my guess: You can't return to shit. But if you never created anything worth returning to...maybe Heaven ain't all that heavenly.

HUSBAND. There has got to be some –

DEAD POLICE CHIEF. Hey, if you see a fucking pamphlet laying around anywhere, pass it the fuck over, obvious'man. They don't give you a map in life, so don't find it all that surprising they make you find your way in death too.

MARI. You listen to me, okay. I do not want your help. I do not want you putting your hands. I do not want anything to do with any of that. Do you understand.

DEAD POLICE CHIEF. Well, then you understand that this is funny position you decided to put yourself in, *Señora Policía*. If you didn't want to be close to any of this, what're you doing so close then?

HUSBAND. We've a daughter.

> (**DEAD POLICE CHIEF** *looks around the house, then looks closely at* **MARI**)

DEAD POLICE CHIEF. *(to* HUSBAND*)* Do you?

HUSBAND. And when she gets here, my wife is right, we can't have anything to do with...

DEAD POLICE CHIEF. Ah, you don't want any *details* close to home, is that it, delusional'man?

HUSBAND. We just don't want any of this anywhere near her –

DEAD POLICE CHIEF. Head?

HUSBAND. ...

DEAD POLICE CHIEF. You are going to be a very caring and careful father, yea.

HUSBAND. Thank you.

DEAD POLICE CHIEF. Weren't a compliment.

MARI. *Señor Policía*, please leave.

DEAD POLICE CHIEF. Do you know what careful is, do you?

HUSBAND. *You're* going to tell me what careful is, really?

MARI. *(to* DPC*)* Did you hear what I said –

DEAD POLICE CHIEF. Careful, will get you exactly a daughter just like you –

HUSBAND. Which is what?

DEAD POLICE CHIEF. Blind to how ugly the world really is. And deaf to even listen at how to change things.

MARI. You leave my house, you leave my family be.

DEAD POLICE CHIEF. You two are worried about images getting into your daughter's thoughts, but let me ask you something: What does your daughter's head really matter, if there ain't a body?

(**DEAD POLICE CHIEF** *puts his head back on.*)

MARI. Go, now.

DEAD POLICE CHIEF. Know this, *Señora Política*: I did not get myself put in two parts because I wasn't careful. It was because I didn't matter. To either side. They don't care, me, I got nobody that care. And what does my life really matter, if nobody care. Whatever you do, Mari, just make sure that at all times, that you are not just being only careful. That what you do matter more than anything. And that people care that you're doing it. Otherwise, they'll take you.

(**DEAD POLICE CHIEF** *opens the door to a stir of music, he walks out into it with wonder, closing the door behind him. However, the music is in the room, in the oxygen, in the sweat on* **MARI** *and* **HUSBAND**. **MARI** *looks around, as though she can see it fulfilling the house,* **HUSBAND** *however begins to move about, it is too much for him. He opens a window for air, but instead is met with a rush of impassioned notes. He steps back from it. He looks at his wife, then rushes to his knees, covering invisible daughter's ears.*)

HUSBAND. It's too much, her little ears, her little receptors…

(to **MIJA***)* "It's okay, huh? They just sounds, Mija.

There's a girl, yea, just breathe easy. See that, your *Papá's* here for you just like always. See how we do that, Mija; we can always go to quiet you an' me.

(Music suffers)

These sounds you hear, these noises in your receptors, Mija…tha's the sound of your *Mamá* not coming home no more."

MARI. Will You Stoppit.

HUSBAND. *(to* MIJA*)* "It was too much for her, Mija. All those sounds out there, your *Mamá* didn't know. She had no idea how much ugly sounds there would be. An' now, now she can't find her way home."

> (MARI *tries to pull* HUSBAND *up; he instinctively protects* MIJA; *they struggle over their invisible daughter.)*

(to MARI*)* You're hurting her.

MARI. What is the matter with you.

HUSBAND. You look at me like that, like how you are, like I can't see straight. But look at what happened to where we live, Mari, look at who you let into where we live. And then you tell me who you're calling sick.

MARI. I call *you* sick.

What kinda father uses his own daughter to –

HUSBAND. *(to* MIJA*)* "No matter what you hear, no matter what you read in the papers, Mija, your *Mamá* was only ever thinking of you."

MARI. You need help, Love.

> (HUSBAND *kisses Mija goodnight, then gets back up)*

HUSBAND. When our daughter comes into this world, I will have already years of love waiting for her. So much of it so that *nothing* will be able to touch her.

MARI. Really? Is that what you think?

HUSBAND. If you didn't believe you or I could protect her then? What did you do all this for?

MARI. What is it that no matter how many times I try an' spill everything-I-have-inside to you, it never sinks. It just washes out into the void that we fuck into calling marriage.

HUSBAND. Lookit you. So strong. So loud. So loud that even the dead know who you are and where we sleep. How long do you think it will be before *los narcos* hear you too?

MARI. We can never get out from under *los narcos* if quiet is the only word we live by. Can't you understand that? People will never be able to get away from men with guns. But if we *live*, if parents keep their children up good, if people do all of this together, *los narcos* will have only guns, but none the men. They will have no generations. Just only this one. And then, finally, there will be an endpoint. *(pause)* Please, tell it to me that you hear me. Please, look at me from out of what's-sick-in-you and remind me why I ever called you Love to begin with. Please.

> *(They share a moment. Music reaches.* **MARI**'s *hand out for* **HUSBAND**. *Beat. He is distracted by the music)*

HUSBAND. I just…

MARI. Tell me. Please. Talk to me. Be here with me.

HUSBAND. …I just don't understand how I'm supposed to think about the future if I have no children in it of my own. *(pause)* And I don't think it's safe for our daughter to be here.

> *(***MARI*** disappoints. Music suffers. Beat.)*

MARI. Be where.

HUSBAND. I'm taking her out of this house.

MARI. So this our house is no longer safe an' you say to me what? That you'll go? That you'll leave me? That I'm alone.

HUSBAND. They'll come for you, Mari. You know that.

MARI. Go on then, go with your sickness out of this house before it infects me.

HUSBAND. What you call sickness, I call our future family.

MARI. I hear you, you know. Speaking to her at all hours, whispering, meeting her out in the yard, laughing with her when you think I'm not noticing. Trying to raise her on your own before she even exists.

> *(***HUSBAND*** begins packing.)*

HUSBAND. So…we'll see you…when? At your funeral, or were you planning on speaking to your family before that? You know, to go over house stuff.

MARI. Look at you. Packing away. So proud to be packing away. So smart. Imagine if every soul in México were as smart as you. Easier to pack their bags, then support by those they say to love. Just the ignorance of so many packed bags across the country, knocking on *Los Estados Unidos* to let them in. The borders lined up.

HUSBAND. Yea, imagine how stupid…people trying for a better life for their family. When they could do like you and just…not have one.

MARI. What you call family I call my loved ones, but what I call family you see as a country of strangers.

HUSBAND. You, me, and our daughter. This is family.

MARI. Congratulations, if that makes you feel like the best father in this entire country, but know this, Love, it also makes you the reason there is no country; entirely.

HUSBAND. Well.

MARI. Aren't you forgetting something?

> (**MARI** *illustrates her midsection.*)

You forgot to say goodbye. She stays here with me, get it?

> (*Beat.* **HUSBAND** *walks to her midsection, bends down; listens.*)

HUSBAND. Hmm…

MARI. What.

HUSBAND. There is absolutely nothing inside there.

> (**HUSBAND** *exits, closing the door behind him. A moment of* **MARI** *with her decision. Lights out.*)

Scene Four

(The exterior of the home. **MARI** *exits, looking up at the morning sun, sounds of a city swell in rhythm with the music. She turns towards the audience nervously and moves towards them; acknowledging them.* **MARI** *smiles politely and gestures knocking on a door; music swells as that door opens.)*

MARI. *Buenas tardes, me llamo Mari, soy la nueva jefa de la policía. ¿Tiene un momento para hablar conmigo?*

(pause)

Gracias. Quería hablarle sobre los niños de nuestra ciudad y sobre cómo todavía se les puede dar una buena educación para asegurarnos de que no –

(Another door, another knock.)

Hola, me llamo Mari. Soy la nueva jefa de la policía. Espero que pueda hablar conmigo unos minutos sobre...

(Another door, another knock. A child answers, **MARI** *reacts, then squats.)*

Wow. ¡Hola! ¿Están tus papás?

)pause)

Oh, no, está bien.

Me llamo Mari. Soy policía. ¿Cómo te llamas?

(pause)

¿Y en dónde están tus papás? ¿En el trabajo?

(pause)

¿Y hay alguien más en casa contigo?

(longer pause)

¿Qué? ¿Qué pasa? ¿Cuál es el problema?

(Stands **EL MORETE**. *Music suffers.)*

Okay, you go back on inside, okay. You go on in the house and shut the door. I'll come again to see you –

EL MORETE. I been *dying* to see you.

MARI. What do you want?

EL MORETE. Lookit you. New Chief of Police an' you working all by your own?

MARI. Yes.

EL MORETE. Me, if I had a wife doing what you're doing, I don't think I could like let her go alone.

MARI. My husband –

EL MORETE. What about him?

MARI. Nevermind.

EL MORETE. You two have a fight or something?

MARI. …

EL MORETE. Es okay. Fighting is like sometimes necessary, yea?

MARI. So, what, you came to see me?

EL MORETE. How you know I ain't come to see him?

MARI. Because my husband's not the Chief of Police, I am.

EL MORETE. Yea, but he's always with you though, no? Waiting outside the station an' shit. Ah, lookit that, who right there. See.

> (**EL MORETE** *points to invisible* **HUSBAND**.)

I can like view him up close now.

> (**EL MORETE** *circles invisible* **HUSBAND**.)

(to invisible **HUSBAND***)* …shit, I bet I could draw you, you know. Draw you in chalk, motherfucker. White chalk. Just be careful, eh, cuz that dust will get on your clothes an' shit. I think I even got a little left on me from the last motherfucker I drew out.

> (**EL MORETE** *stares invisible* **HUSBAND** *down*.)

(to **MARI***)* Hey, Policía, I hate to like get involved between a husband and wife, but your husband…do you see he crying. *(pause)* Es okay, here, lemme see what I can do. I talk to him, you know like two men talking.

> (**EL MORETE** *motions he needs a moment*.)

(**EL MORETE** *has the murmuring of a chat with invisible* **HUSBAND**. *He finishes.*)

Okay *Policía*. I had a little chat with him, and I'm just gonna tell you where he at with things, okay? So your husband, he believe that you should go. That you should run. Like right now. Like a pussy. Away from me. But what your husband don't know...is that pussy *never* run away from me.

MARI. How can I help you?

EL MORETE. You can help me to see the station.

MARI. Why.

EL MORETE. Are you allowed to ask me that? Isn't the police station like a public institution or whatever? Isn't a station like my rights and privileges?

It's right up this way, no?

(**EL MORETE** *leads* **MARI** *and invisible* **HUSBAND** *to the station. Upon entering the station,* **EL MORETE** *begins looking about.*)

You know if you're going to use the word station, there really oughta be a lot more people? I think station, I think like...busy. Like you should see the bus station. It *feels* like a station, you know.

(*to invisible* **HUSBAND**) You know what I'm talkin'about right, *puto*?

MARI. So what is it you – ?

EL MORETE. So where is everybody? Your fellow officers. The ones that you're the chief of.

MARI. They're out in the community, talking to –

(**EL MORETE** *spots the car radio.*)

That's a –

(**EL MORETE** *picks up the car radio, he listens. Flicks the dials, which do nothing. He shows to invisible* **HUSBAND**.)

EL MORETE. *(to invisible* **HUSBAND***)* You believe this shit, *puto?* Like if you had to guess, man to man, why you think this radio, that ain't attached to nothin', is like… sounding?

> *(He listens as though getting a response.)*

Yea…mmm hmm…yea tha's a good point, puto.

(to **MARI***)* You know what your husband say? He say that this radio making the sound, is like not good. That you should bust it open, just put a hammer to it till it don't sound no more.

MARI. It's just a found item.

EL MORETE. Found where.

MARI. Was one of my officers recovered it.

EL MORETE. For realz? So you never used this radio yourself, you never like handled it?

MARI. One of my officers recovered it, and placed it on that table there. And now you're handling it. That's its entire history. What is it you want.

EL MORETE. See, I was in a junkyard kinda…parking lot, a couple days ago. And there was a car radio there, an' this car radio, well it worked like…wha'cha'ma'callit, "surround sound," yea? This sound was like… surrounding us. You know surround sound?

(to invisible **HUSBAND***)* Do she? Do she know surround sound?

MARI. I do.

EL MORETE. Es scary, huh?

MARI. I'm okay with it.

EL MORETE. *(to invisible* **HUSBAND***)* Is she? Okay with it?

MARI. Did you really come here to talk about electronics?

EL MORETE. No, I came here to report about wha'happen in that junkyard fucking parking lot. I came here to report about the sound that surrounded that whole entire shit.

MARI. You wish to report a noise violation?

EL MORETE. Yea, I guess you could say I was pretty "violated," like in here.

(He taps his head.)

MARI. Okay, just fill this out for me and –

(She hands him a form, he stares at it.)

EL MORETE. What do you expect me to do with that?

MARI. You take this pen, you take the cap off, you put the pen downward towards the paper with the little inkball facing out, you –

EL MORETE. *(to invisible* **HUSBAND** *)* You best tell your woman that I don't know what she expects me to do with some shit ass piece of paper? She gonna take it over to her non'existent clerk and –

MARI. What is it you would want to happen?

EL MORETE. *(to invisible* **HUSBAND** *)* What I want is for her to take this car radio and switch the switch to on.

(He hands her the radio)

That little dial there. To the right.

MARI. I'm not allowed to get prints on the –

*(***EL MORETE*** points a gun at invisible* **HUSBAND** *)*

EL MORETE. How about for your invisible husband tho'?

(A moment. She takes the car radio, the lights of the station flicker.)

Now, change the station.

MARI. I don't understand what –

*(***EL MORETE*** clicks the gun. She switches the station, ***EL MORETE****'s sister's ass fills the room. ***EL MORETE*** startles, almost dropping the gun. He looks around the room, opens a window: music is heard)*

EL MORETE. Outside, go.

(She goes, he follows.)

Alright, where the fuck is it playing from?

MARI. I don't know.

EL MORETE. It's not just cars; I can hear it from…

MARI. I'm telling you I have no idea –

EL MORETE. …it's coming from the houses. An' from those stores right there. It's coming from every'fucking'where in the city.

MARI. I'm sorry.

EL MORETE. *And* this song's a piece of shit, whys it gotta be this song?

MARI. Look, I don't know anything.

EL MORETE. Turn it off.

MARI. Okay…

EL MORETE. I said turn the music to fucking off.

> *(***EL MORETE*** grabs the radio, turns the dial: nothing. He begins shaking the radio like a small boy.)*

Turn Off, You Fucking Piece Of Shit.

> *(***EL MORETE*** tires himself out, then humbly hands the radio to ***MARI****; she turns the dial, music softens but remains.)*

MARI. I'm not an electrician okay, I –

EL MORETE. Alright, firstly:

> *(He signs of the cross.)*

thank you I'm not crazy.

Fucking nobody believed me about that lot. They laughed in my face an' shit. An' now, whenever anybody walks by me, they start humming that fucking song. I'm fucking getting picked on. I fucking have a gun; I shouldn't be getting picked on!

MARI. It's just some glitch or –

EL MORETE. Yea, your face is a glitch.

MARI. …how is my face a –

EL MORETE. Hey, shut up. I'm trying to like process. Es not every day some magic car radio –

MARI. It's not a magic car radio.

EL MORETE. No? It is a car radio, yea?

MARI. Yea.

EL MORETE. And it works like *magically* different from all other car radios, yea?

MARI. Yes.

EL MORETE. So it's a magic'fucking'car radio then! Now will you just shut up so I can process.

MARI. Is this why you came here, you wanted to investigate the magic car radio?

EL MORETE. *(to invisible* **HUSBAND***)* Hey, tell you wife if she don't shut up, I'm gonna investigate that dumpster over there with her body.

MARI. ...how would you use my body to investigate a dumpster? You'd have to carry me all the way over there, then lift me up and what? Wave me around... investigating...maybe I could make a little beeping sound like one of those detectors. Beep...beep... beep...

(**EL MORETE** *moves in on her.*)

Beepbeepbeep, yer getting closer.

(**EL MORETE** *pulls his gun.*)

EL MORETE. *(to invisible* **HUSBAND***)* On your knees, puto.

(**EL MORETE** *points down at invisible* **HUSBAND.***)

(to **MARI***)* See how easy he do like I say? A man shouldn't be so easy to tell what to do, but I guess, he, your husband, he do whatever, huh?

MARI. I haven't done anything to you. I was just trying to –

EL MORETE. To what.

MARI. I'm sorry; you were processing.

EL MORETE. I'm through.

MARI. Okay.

EL MORETE. *(to invisible* **HUSBAND***)* Now, *puto*, unless you want your wife to see your insides just all over the fucking place: where did she get this radio?

MARI. My officer recovered –

EL MORETE. *(to invisible* **HUSBAND***)* An' if she think I'm going to like just let all this go, she got like a lifetime of things to rethink, don't she, *puto*.

MARI. If I could answer your question, don't you think I would?

EL MORETE. *(to invisible* **HUSBAND***)* Me, no. I think that your wife will never answer me my questions, I think she think that if she just play like stupid, that nobody will be looking at her. But re'think about this, puto, if your wife doesn't smash that car radio like right fucking now…

>   (**EL MORETE** *pulls his mobile phone.*)

Everybody Will Be Looking At Her.

>   *(A moment of* **MARI** *holding the car radio, looking at it;* **EL MORETE** *waiting for her.*)

(to **MARI***)* What're you scared for, Mari? Es just a found item, no?

>   (**EL MORETE***'s phone rings, it startles him, he drops it then quickly recovers and answers; lights darkens over him.* **MARI** *stands alone, we see fear underneath the surface for the first time. Lights return to* **EL MORETE.***)*

(to phone) Sí, sí, yo entiendo.

>   *(He hangs up obediently.)*

(to **MARI***)* Next time I see you, Mari,

MARI. Who was that?

EL MORETE. Nevermind your ass who was that.

MARI. Okay…

EL MORETE. Next time I see you, that car radio better be…

MARI. Gone.

EL MORETE. Dusted. Cuz if it ain't, I'll know about it an' guess what.

MARI. How will you know about it?

EL MORETE. Because I have fucking hearing. *An' guess what.*

MARI. What?

> (**EL MORETE** *pushes invisible* **HUSBAND** *over to the floor.*)

EL MORETE. Do you see how easy he push over?

MARI. …

EL MORETE. Do you?

MARI. Yes.

EL MORETE. Yea, we do too.

> (**EL MORETE** *exits into darkness.* **MARI** *walks to invisible* **HUSBAND**, *she kneels, touching where his body would be, then speaks to somebody younger.*)

MARI. *(to* **MIJA***)* "He'll be okay, Mija, don't you worry, huh? See that, he's just resting that's all."

> (*She pets his head and she lies beside him, her head on his chest; she begins to weep with her invisible family. A few moments. She sits up, listens, the music is faint, almost non-existent.* **MARI** *begins to hum, the humming turns to more. Strength finds her. She continues her own sound until the notes of the music resume. She looks up, listening. Humbled.*)

> (*A few moments. She gets up and dusts herself off before returning to the station. She begins confidently to fill out reports then hand them to clerks who are not there, assign equipment then hand off to officers who cannot be seen. Music builds as the does this, she finds her rhythm. Her movements find their way to dance, to true beauty.* **MARI** *looks like progress.* **MARI** *looks around her as reports begin to file themselves, as equipment hands*)

itself off. The light outside turns to beautiful. The station looks like what the world should be like.)

(Time stops. The station portraits. **MARI** *looks at the landscape of what she has created in awe. We are in the space of human progress.)*

(Lights reveal **DEAD POLICE CHIEF** *with bloodied hands. He looks like the afterwards of violence. His hands shake.* **DEAD POLICE CHIEF** *removes his head embarrassed.)*

DEAD POLICE CHIEF. Thank you for calling me back, *Señora Polícia.*

MARI. What is this, I didn't call –

> *(***DEAD POLICE CHIEF*** *shows his shaking bloodied hands.)*

DEAD POLICE CHIEF. Cuz do you see, under my nails, tha's what any motherfucker with a gun look like, tha's what kinda red they blood.

MARI. What're you doing here with that, I told you not to bring –

DEAD POLICE CHIEF. *Señora Polícia,* I put my hands on so many of *los narcos...*

> *(***DEAD POLICE CHIEF*** *stresses his hands into strangulation, then into tearing and clawing, into absolute madness.)*

an' now lookit me, anything ever good in me... I strangled it out...

MARI. You stupid man, look at me, look at where we're at now. Don't you see, this is not a place of bodies no more.

DEAD POLICE CHIEF. I kill so many of these men, these men who answer to their mobiles every day. But they only fight with each other more. They don't know my killing from their killing. It was all just killing.

MARI. There is no more of that. Do you understand me –

DEAD POLICE CHIEF. You see, *los narcos,* they just answer'to. But, *Señora Polícia,* if I can find my way to those *other* men who never just answer'to; if I can follow my way across *La Linea* an' look back at you from *Los Estados Unidos.* Then I will have my good again.

> (**DEAD POLICE CHIEF** *points north*)

Look up there, *Señora Polícia,* just past our border, can't you see them so close. They have the kinda bodies we need.

MARI. I don't see bodies, past our border. I see only people walking, people smiling at their everyday. I see them laugh while you an' I are here not laughing. I want to laugh. But how do we get there, huh? Without using our hands. Without anymore bodies. How can they hear us what we sound like just as easy as we can hear them how they laugh?

> (**MARI** *begins to hum,* **DEAD POLICE CHIEF** *listens with abandon. Humming turns to song.* **MARI** *lets words out. Beauty graces the world around them. What was dead now seems alive. The world comes to color from dust.*)

Scene Five

(Center on **GÜERO** *who stands listening to the music; trying to place it. He texts. From across the way,* **EL MORETE** *walks up, glares at him. A few moments of this.)*

GÜERO. Alright, what is it? Is it the music, so you're feeling romantic, and that's how come you can't take your eyes off?

EL MORETE. What?

GÜERO. You're staring. Which I'm used to, don't get me wrong. But a little tip from me to you, when you're gonna stare at somebody, you can't like actually stare at them. You have to stand at some sort of angle, or behind a bush, mailbox maybe, a small boy perhaps. And then what you do is:

*(***GÜERO*** *poses like a bar checking people out.)*

See now did you see that? I just did a complete once'over an' I did it without looking all...y'know, creepy.

EL MORETE. What are you doing here, Güero???

GÜERO. Why I'm here for you.

EL MORETE. Hey, Güero, if yer meaning my dick, there's two things:

One, don't you ever fucking mean my dick!

Two, you couldn't afford it.

GÜERO. Okay, that's a weird response, but –

EL MORETE. But what.

GÜERO. Well, one, if I *was* meaning your dick wouldn't that mean I'm like a bottom? Isn't that how it works? Anyways, lookit me. I'm such a fucking top it's ridiculous. And two, if there is anywhere I could afford any dick I want, it'd be down here in Mexico, am I right?

EL MORETE. You do realize I'm the one with the gun, right?

GÜERO. You do realize I'm the one with the money, right?

EL MORETE. You stupid or something?

GÜERO. Something.

EL MORETE. I'm the one with the gun, *thus* I'm the one with your money.

GÜERO. You are talking about shooting me for the money in my wallet, yes?

EL MORETE. I don't need the gun for that, Güero.

GÜERO. Yea, but then how would you get the money that's *not* in my wallet, wet...back.

EL MORETE. The only reason I'm not like beating the shit outta you right now is cuz –

GÜERO. I'm bigger than you?

EL MORETE. I'm bigger.

GÜERO. Then why do you need a gun.

EL MORETE. I don't need a gun, I just like them.

GÜERO. I like tits, I don't carry them around with me.

EL MORETE. Tha's cuz you can't.

GÜERO. No, really, I wouldn't carry them around with me. That's weird. Besides...

EL MORETE. What.

GÜERO. Is it just in the States, or do tits get boring after awhile? I mean getting to'em is nice, but once you've gotten there...they lack longevity.

EL MORETE. No.

GÜERO. No what?

EL MORETE. Es not just a States thing, they get like that here too.

GÜERO. How did we get to talking about this?

EL MORETE. Eh, I said I like guns and you said you wouldn't carry tits around with you.

GÜERO. What were we talking about before guns an' tits then?

EL MORETE. Hey, shit, what else is there, huh?!

> (**EL MORETE** *makes for a high five.* **GÜERO** *looks at him oddly,* **EL MORETE** *retreats his hand.*)

GÜERO. That was awkward.

EL MORETE. Was just a high five.

GÜERO. You did hear when I said I didn't like dick, right? I mean just because I get bored with tits doesn't mean –

EL MORETE. Hey, it was a high five, so why don't you shut up.

GÜERO. What were we talking about before you wanted to hold hands.

(EL MORETE *pulls his gun.*)

EL MORETE. We were talking about the money that's not in your wallet, Güero.

GÜERO. Oh that, yea.

EL MORETE. That, yea.

GÜERO. Of course, that.

EL MORETE. Fuckin'that.

GÜERO. Will you stop flirting –

EL MORETE. You got a lotta balls talkin'to me –

GÜERO. Is it me, or do you keep making veiled homosexual references –

EL MORETE. I'm'bout to veil you in a fucking coffin, Güero.

GÜERO. *Veil* me in a *coffin?*

EL MORETE. What about the money that's not in your wallet; where is it then?

GÜERO. Well, it's in a bank; in the States. You think I'd bring it down to *Mexico?*

EL MORETE. So wha'd you bring it up for then?

(*beat*)

GÜERO. What's with the music anyways?

EL MORETE. ...es like uncomforting, huh?

GÜERO. Is it always this...obvious?

EL MORETE. No. Not always.

(GÜERO *looks up at the music,* EL MORETE *joins.*)

GÜERO. ...I bet you do this with all the boys.

> (**EL MORETE** *re'points the gun.*)

EL MORETE. Hey, enough, no more distracting.

GÜERO. I sincerely hope this isn't the same tone of customer service your plaza provides on a daily basis.

> (*beat*)

EL MORETE. …ahh shit…yo *entiendo*.

> (**EL MORETE** *pulls a small baggie of white.*)

…why didn't you just say? How much, Güero, gimme a number.

GÜERO. You don't know who I am, do you.

EL MORETE. You don't know who *I* am.

GÜERO. No, really, you should get on your little phone there and ask somebody higher up about who I am.

EL MORETE. Look, I ain't doin'no specials, just tell me how much you –

GÜERO. Really, you think I'm like haggling money with you?

EL MORETE. Bitch, I make more money than you ever –

GÜERO. Oh, is that how it works, they let you keep the money?

EL MORETE. *Familia.*

GÜERO. Excuse me, did you just say *familia?*

EL MORETE. What I make, we make.

GÜERO. That's… adorable.

EL MORETE. How much?

GÜERO. You're really more of a reactionary guy, aren't you? Here, why don't you react to this:

> (**EL MORETE** *confuses.* **GÜERO** *pulls his mobile phone, he scrolls through his contacts, then shows one of them to* **EL MORETE,** *who reacts fumbling his gun, which* **GÜERO** *takes with ease.*)

Wow. You sweat a lot, huh? It's all…greasy.

EL MORETE. Gimme.

GÜERO. First you say Gimme a Number, then you say Gimme the gun. Do I have to give you everything? Can't you get anything on your own? You know what you are?

(**EL MORETE** *pulls his mobile.*)

EL MORETE. Gimme the gun back or I'll dial.

GÜERO. You're needy. Hasn't anybody ever told you how unattractive needy is? You're never gonna get that good dick by bein'needy. It's a turn off.

EL MORETE. I'm dialing.

GÜERO. "Hi, boss'man, can you send my lieutenant over, I lost my gun to a gringo and he won't *gimme* it back."

EL MORETE. I won't shoot you if you gimme the gun back.

GÜERO. …alright, alright, you've got me, I'll give you the gun back, but only on the condition that you don't shoot me.

(**GÜERO** *holds his hands up, waiting for the shot.*)

EL MORETE. They won't let you take the gun past customs.

GÜERO. …

EL MORETE. Shut up, it just came out.

GÜERO. Did you used to work for U.S. Customs or something because let me tell you something, you are right on the money! It's like you read their handbook or maybe you just think alike, but there is something going on with your brain and the Department of Customs and Border Protection, they're like…in sync.

EL MORETE. Sometimes I say shit I don't think about. Are you going to give me my gun back or not?

GÜERO. Is it *your* gun, I mean, did you buy it? With your own money, or is this more like a *familia* gun.

EL MORETE. Why you wanna embarrass me, huh?

GÜERO. You pointed a gun at me.

EL MORETE. Yea, but tha's sorta like my job an' shit.

GÜERO. Well then maybe its sorta like my job an' shit to embarrass you.

EL MORETE. Look, I didn't buy the gun, they gave it to me. An' if you don't think I'm embarrassed already enough for my fucking life, then you're not looking at me very closely, Güero. An' I ain't even talking about today. Me, I'm embarrassed for everything that I do. I don't do anything right. So like you, standing there, making me a fool for the day, is like…not original.

GÜERO. So if I give you the gun, will you dial on your little prepaid phone there and please just tell your lieutenant who you're here with?

EL MORETE. Wait, who *am* I here with?

GÜERO. You get sidetracked a lot, don't you. Not a good characteristic in the field so much, is it.

> (**GÜERO** *puts the gun back in* **EL MORETE***'s hand. Just as both their hands are on the gun equally, lights reveal* **MARI***.*)

MARI. …Freeze…!

> (*They do. Lights shift,* **MARI** *cautiously walks closer to the two frozen men with a gun connecting them. She looks at them as though she is looking at a human heart out of the body and pumping just in front of her. A few moments, disrupted by* **DEAD POLICE CHIEF***, who enters with a shotgun.*)

I didn't think, I just saw them, I –

DEAD POLICE CHIEF. Lookit that, an Americano right put here for us.

MARI. What do I do?

DEAD POLICE CHIEF. What all *policía* do in this our country: what we have to.

> (**DEAD POLICE CHIEF** *cracks his knuckles.*)

So, which one first, light or dark?

MARI. No, neither, I –

DEAD POLICE CHIEF. What do you think men like this will react to your –

MARI. I don't know, I –

DEAD POLICE CHIEF. *Señora Polícia,* this is exactly the bodies our country need.

MARI. No. No killing, absolutely –

DEAD POLICE CHIEF. I am sorry, but sometimes there *is absolutely* killing.

MARI. ...El Morete, he's just a hawk, and who knows what this other guy, they're probably just lower level –

DEAD POLICE CHIEF. You an' I both know ain't no more lower nada. What was once underground is on the streets.

MARI. What are they even doing here? They don't even look like, I mean look at them...

DEAD POLICE CHIEF. *Dime.* Tell me what you see, Mari, say to me what your sound look like.

> (**DEAD POLICE CHIEF** *begins to hum, as* **MARI** *had. As* **MARI** *talks the music overwhelms; her emotion floods)*

MARI. Es like they're not just two men no more, d'you know? These are not just two men standing in the street, with a weapon out the open. Look at how the weight of their bodies, pushing against with just force. No letting up, no moving with. See how their eyes don't look straight; no they dart everywhere but actually at each other. Their hearts pumping out of sync. And the way they breathe close up, trying to measure out what the other will do next. And there is no closeness, just only one out'manning the other. One trying to be as strong as the other. And two right like beside each other but behaving as though they are atmospheres apart.

When I look at these two men... I see the closing of civilization and the stopping of babies being born. I see people and disappearance. I see nothing left but the vacancy of human connection for the catastrophe of countries.

DEAD POLICE CHIEF. And what do you want to do to them?

MARI. ...I wish it I could just keep them frozen like this. I wish it I could reach in an' just pull the gun from between them. And when they wake...they will have no idea what they were doing so at ends.

> (DEAD POLICE CHIEF *positions the shotgun in* MARI's *hands, in proper formation.*)

DEAD POLICE CHIEF. And what can you do in the real world, Mari, here, now? My guess: you can do things I cannot even imagine...but in order to do them, Mari, you need to speak their language. C'mon...

> (DEAD POLICE CHIEF *begins to position* MARI *down on one knee, with the shotgun pointed.*)

You know you can't reach your un'armed hand between them and try to fuck with what they have in common. Cuz if you do, they'll only pull you in, they'll incorporate you. But listen to *la música*, Mari, *la música* says it that you have more power in you than these two men can even see; and that if you use it, they will do whatever it is you want...

> (MARI *takes her position, her aim on* EL MORETE *and* GÜERO.)

Yes. Lookit you. *You* are what this country needs. What I never was. Go on. You don't need me for this, this is who you are.

MARI. *(to* EL MORETE *and* GÜERO) I SAID FREEZE.

> (*The weight of* MARI *wakes the two men. All three look at each other. Lights out. End of Act I*)

ACT TWO

Scene One

*(Right where we left off. **MARI** on one knee, shotgun pointed. **GÜERO** raises his hand.)*

GÜERO. So, what happens if we don't freeze?

MARI. Mister, shut up and don't talk.

GÜERO. Do I have to do both? How about if I shut up, but I still talk. Would that work?

MARI. I want you both to lower the gun, then step away. Slowly. Do all of this slowly.

GÜERO. What if we do *some* of it slowly?

MARI. I'm not going to arrest anybody; I'm not even going to ask questions. I just –

EL MORETE. You ain't goin'arrest nobody, you ain't goin'ask questions, then what the fuck you even doing here then?

MARI. …

GÜERO. I think what my little friend is trying to ask here is: are you screaming at us to freeze as an officer of the law…or just some broad? Cuz I gotta tell you, a lady officer tellin'me to stay put is a hell of a lot different than a woman who wants me to hold still.

MARI. I am telling you both right now, to lower the gun. That is the only directive you need right now.

(They lower the gun more, but take their time.)

EL MORETE. I don't think your husband will be very happy about this; you told him you wouldn't interfere, but here you are –

MARI. We're putting down the gun, that's all we're doing.

EL MORETE. C'mon, you'member. You were laying in bed when you promised it. He was on your right with that little lamp shut, you were on his left with your light still lit.

GÜERO. What're you stalking her? I thought you liked dick.

EL MORETE. I'm'bout to stock you with dick.

(*GÜERO stares at* **EL MORETE.**)

It just came out! I like women. I like tits.

(*The gun is on the ground.* **MARI** *strategically picks the gun up. She wipes the handle.*)

GÜERO. Yea, it's all greasy, right?

EL MORETE. Yo, even with a fuckin'sawed'off shotgun you still gotta make the fun?

GÜERO. It isn't sawed'off.

EL MORETE. It might as fuckin'well be, it's pointed at us.

GÜERO. Do you like think at all, or do you just run on batteries?

EL MORETE. Alright, you've got the gun, *Polícia*. Congratulations. How very Chief of you. Now can we go?

MARI. Go where.

EL MORETE. To finish what we got to finish.

MARI. Which is what?

EL MORETE. I thought you didn't wanna know my business, *Polícia*, but here you are all up in it.

MARI. I'm not in it –

EL MORETE. Look at you. Standing there with that shotgun in your hands, stopping what I do, stopping what he do. Shit, you are so in it, Mari, the smell of your pussy is like flavoring this whole entire transaction.

(MARI reactively steps in and butts the base of her gun to EL MORETE's head, he drops. She composes.)

GÜERO. Interesting.

MARI. I can't believe I just –

GÜERO. You know though?

MARI. What.

GÜERO. You can't take that back. That right there is what we call permanence.

MARI. He isn't anybody.

GÜERO. True. But c'mon, we're all somebody. Right? Inside.

MARI. What're you doing out here, Güero.

GÜERO. Hey, what do I know, I just follow him.

MARI. Really? You follow him? This little one?

EL MORETE. Alright, first of all. Fucking OW. Secondly, if you fucking people don't stop calling me little –

(EL MORETE gets up.)

And thirdly, Mari, you've no idea what you just –

GÜERO. Are you forgetting something?

EL MORETE. What?

GÜERO. Oh, you know, If She Shoots You, Nobody Will Know, or care, That You Got Hit In The Head.

EL MORETE. Why you gotta reduce everything?

GÜERO. *(to MARI)* I'm sorry about that. You were…

MARI. *(to GÜERO)* You know, when he talks, I understand where he lands in things,

EL MORETE. Hey, I don't *land* in things. I *am* things.

(GÜERO gives an 'I don't know what to do with him' look.)

MARI. but when *you* talk, Güero, you sound like you come from somewhere…

GÜERO. As opposed to…nowhere?

MARI. Yes.

EL MORETE. Yo, what the fuck are you two even talking about?

MARI. What is it you have to finish? Who are you?

GÜERO. Well, *I*, was trying to convince the little guy here –

EL MORETE. I hate you.

GÜERO. That he should pick up his little flip phone there and make a phone call to his lieutenant letting them know just what sort of gringo he found wandering –

MARI. And just what sort of gringo did he find wandering?

GÜERO. Well, the charming sort mostly. But I'm also tired.

MARI. Tired from what?

GÜERO. Well, traveling. And all the fucking I do. Handsome, white man's burden.

MARI. What business do you have to finish.

GÜERO. You ever heard of a rendezvous point?

MARI. Yes.

GÜERO. Well, that's just movie bullshit, nobody actually has those anymore. I mean we've got cell phones.

MARI. Why are you here, Güero.

GÜERO. Because. I heard there was this really very impressive twenty-two year old criminology student who up an' volun'fucking'teeered to be the new Chief of Police in some little town. Right here in Mexico.

EL MORETE. Wait, what…???

GÜERO. So if I may, Mari, ask what it is that *you* are doing here?

MARI. …

GÜERO. This is an appealing town. Not like, aesthetically maybe, but there is something…

> (**GÜERO** *begins to walk in on* **MARI**, *who backs away.*)

Oh, an' El Morete, make your fucking call.

> (**EL MORETE** *dials, darkness falls over him.*)

MARI. Stop right there.

GÜERO. It's nice, isn't it. When you go from three to two. Me, I was always better talking with just two. Three...it complicates.

MARI. What about me? So you heard about me and now you're here to what?

GÜERO. What I heard, was that you were a very peaceful volunteer. No firearms. No drug arrests. Just "community building." Is that the term? Community building. *(pause)* No, really, is it?

MARI. Yes.

GÜERO. And I don't know, I imagine community building, well, I guess I just picture like an' actual building within the community. Probably fairs an' shit on the weekends. *(pause)* What? No fairs?

MARI. You come all the way down here to –

GÜERO. To find that you're really not as peaceful as all that really. I mean look at you, you've a bigger gun than even him.

*(Lights resume over **EL MORETE**.)*

*(to **EL MORETE**)* God, I missed you.

EL MORETE. Alright. I tol'em.

GÜERO. You didn't miss me?

EL MORETE. Do you wanna know what they tol'me or no?

GÜERO. Y'know I like that you're asking me permission. Keep that.

EL MORETE. I'll text it.

*(**EL MORETE** begins texting.)*

...Wha's yer number.

*(**GÜERO** shows **EL MORETE** his number, who then sends.)*

GÜERO. *(to **MARI**)* His manners are... This'll just take a...

*(**GÜERO** reads the text. **EL MORETE** watches him read it intently. **GÜERO** shrugs.)*

*(to **EL MORETE**)* You know, you spelled "execute" wrong.

(**EL MORETE** *quickly re'looks at his phone.*)

GÜERO. (*to* **MARI**, *laughing*) I'm just…fucking with him. (*pause*) He didn't really spell it wrong.

(**MARI** *re'raises the shotgun.*)

MARI. Enough. Both of you, your phones to the ground, then kick them towards me.

GÜERO. *Kick* them? Couldn't we just hand them to you. Toss maybe?

MARI. On the ground.

EL MORETE. Shit is done, *policía*, even if you like shot us both right now, our location is already noted.

MARI. You drop your fucking phone, or how would you like me to drop you again.

(**EL MORETE** *tosses his phone at* **MARI**'s *feet, she scoops it up; wipes*)

Now yours.

GÜERO. …it's just, his is like cheap an' whatever, mine's is –

MARI. Give it to me.

(**GÜERO** *walks in on* **MARI**, *his phone held out*)

GÜERO. It's just not the sort of phone one can be careless with.

(**MARI** *tries to maneuver reaching out for the phone. When both their hands are on the phone…*)

Do you have kids?

(**MARI** *takes the phone, then re'maneuvers her shotgun.*)

MARI. Why did you ask me that.

GÜERO. Because you're a woman.

EL MORETE. Okay, you've the gun, you've our phones –

GÜERO. You've got all the information that you need, its right there in your hands. But how are you gonna read what's in those phones, though, Mari? You'd have to let either us or the shotgun go.

EL MORETE. Or you could just shoot us. I bet that would like solve all your problems, huh?

(**MARI** *pumps the shotgun, aims downwards.*)

GÜERO. Very nicely thought out, Mari. A couple leg'shots would be very fitting here.

EL MORETE. Hey. Mari, so like whoever taught you how to handle that piece must think an awful lot uh you. That's how a *man* handles it. Cuz his shoulders are thick enough to like absorb the kick. But with your frame an' shit, if you were to plug one of us in the leg, that weapon would kickback so fucking much that it'd prolly knock you flat. Prolly bust up your shoulder bones an' shit. And while you scream, one of us will just pick that piece up. And aim the other plug straight at you.

(**EL MORETE** *places his hand on the barrel.*)

MARI. …I'll do it…

EL MORETE. This ain't you, Mari. This us.

(**MARI** *aims up and fires a shot, the shotgun kicks back into her shoulder, knocking her to the floor just as* **EL MORETE** *described.* **EL MORETE** *and* **GÜERO** *look a bit in shock at the turn of events. The color of the world fades, sounds of gunfire in the background, what was alive now feels dead*)

(*to* **GÜERO**) Yo, who the fuck called that shit? I Did.

(**GÜERO** *looks at him; disappoints, then picks up the shotgun with ease. They look down at* **MARI** *who embarrasses in pain; trying to hold back tears.*)

GÜERO. Well. Maybe I didn't really need to come down here after all. Ah, what am I saying, I love it down here. It's so…and you meet the funniest little people.

EL MORETE. Hey, I fucking called it, yo. So why don't you call me with some fucking respect.

GÜERO. Has anyone ever told you how similar you are to a woman?

EL MORETE. Has anyone ever told you how similar *you* are to a...clown?

GÜERO. ...Is that a reference to my pale complexion or to my sense of humor? Either way, I'm proud of both; equally.

EL MORETE. You're a clown because you treat everybody like children, even people who fucking helped you.

GÜERO. *You* helped *me?*

EL MORETE. YES.

GÜERO. Alright, now you're getting emotional.

EL MORETE. I'm through talking to you.

GÜERO. Oh, c'mon, but you're so interesting.

EL MORETE. Do you ever take anything seriously?

GÜERO. Only your eyes, when I feel them on me.

> (**MARI** *begins to hum to herself. All stop and look at her.*)

EL MORETE. Yo, she goin'crazy or what.

GÜERO. Don't you have somewhere you have to be?

EL MORETE. Wha's with the humming anyways, that like a signal or something? *(pause)* Hey, if you got some like... whatever, you could like let me in on it. *(pause)* What? Oh I ain't smart enough to –

Oh. OH. Shit, why didn't you just say. No judge from me. Man needs what man needs.

GÜERO. And what is that.

EL MORETE. What.

GÜERO. What man needs.

EL MORETE. Hey, like I said, no judge. You do what you gotta.

GÜERO. And what is it you think I gotta.

EL MORETE. What, you want me to like act it out for you, maricon?

GÜERO. No. I don't want you to act it out for me. Because you haven't the first fucking clue as what to act like. How to behave. So why don't do what you do best and take a fucking order.

EL MORETE. What the shit is up your ass? *(pause)* Hey, you know what, fuck this shit.

(**EL MORETE** *makes to storm off.*)

GÜERO. You forgetting something?

EL MORETE. What is there something you wanna hear me say so you can make the fun again, huh? What am I forgetting, am I forgetting your dick in my ass, huh, you tell me what the fuck forgetting, you moody fuck.

(**GÜERO** *reaches into* **MARI**'s *person and pulls the phones, he tosses* **EL MORETE**'s *on the floor; who embarrassingly picks it up.*)

GÜERO. Or did you forget just how meaningless you are without that.

(**EL MORETE** *exits.* **GÜERO** *looks down at* **MARI** *carefully; listening to her.*)

That's quite a...hum. *(pause)* Now is that something you went to school or...no, no school, I understand. Well, alright, I'm not about to say I understand, whatever it is you're doing down there, Mari, but –

(*Enter* **DEAD POLICE CHIEF** *with a rush; just as* **GÜERO** *turns to see what the noise,* **DEAD POLICE CHIEF** *grabs him violently and pulls him off from* **MARI**; *he looks up in shock as* **DEAD POLICE CHIEF** *moves in on him.*)

MARI. No, let him up. Hey. Let him up.

(**MARI** *goes to* **DEAD POLICE CHIEF**)

Listen, *Señor Policía,* do you hear? LISTEN.

(**MARI** *puts his attention to the suffering music, they both listen.*)

MARI. Now take your gun, you take these weapons and you go. Do you hear me? Do you hear what my music sound like?

DEAD POLICE CHIEF. I only wanted my good again

MARI. Look at me. Look at him. Does this look like good to you?

DEAD POLICE CHIEF. I don't know what this look like. You on the floor, this Americano. I don't know what to think, what to do, so I...

MARI. Your hands are shaking, *Señor.* You're scared. So am I. Did you know that?

DEAD POLICE CHIEF. I don't know what I know no more.

MARI. Me either. I don't know what about any of this. But listen to *la música, Señor.* That is all what I'm doing. Now you go. And take these, there are no more of these we want in our country.

> (*She references weapons, but doesn't touch. She hums, he listens, then joins as he gathers the weapons, then exits.* **GÜERO** *gets up, dusts himself off.*)

GÜERO. Well. That was...cultural. So he comes around during all months, not just October?

MARI. Hey, Americano. You follow with me, huh.

GÜERO. *Me follow with you???* What am I –

MARI. You followed me from your country to mine, this is what you do, no? So...then do what they pay you to do an' shut up about it.

> (**MARI** *leads* **GÜERO** *to the station. Upon entering, she pulls the car radio and places it in front of him.* **GÜERO** *stares at the radio sounding.*)

Go on. I know you want to.

> (*He picks up the radio with care. A moment.*)

GÜERO. Do you know what I like best about this thing?

MARI. You tell me.

GÜERO. It's the knobs. They're so simple. You got one for the volume, and one for the station. They got a buncha other shit on'em now, but what more do you need, right? Volume and station.

(GÜERO turns the nobs gently: nothing.)

MARI. You touch it like you touch a woman: with no response.

GÜERO. Hey, easy there, chica, I'm married.

MARI. You don't look married.

GÜERO. Thank you.

MARI. You look very singular to me.

GÜERO. Well, I'm not. Married, that is.

MARI. So you're a liar.

(GÜERO sets the radio down carefully.)

So what do you know about that, huh? The music.

GÜERO. Well it was invented in –

MARI. It's coming from our microwave, from our refrigerator, alarm clock. That radio isn't even connected to anything. What do you know about the music, Güero.

GÜERO. That's funny.

MARI. What is?

GÜERO. I followed you all the way south to ask you that very same question, Mari.

MARI. …

GÜERO. C'mon, smart woman like you must have a hunch.

MARI. It's nothing. Some glitch. You?

GÜERO. I'm just a tourist.

MARI. Hunch then.

(He moves in on MARI, speaking with a severity of him that we've not seen before.)

GÜERO. …Well…if you want my honest…fucking… thoughts on the matter, Mari…on the music… I'd say that something completely…fucking…incredible must be behind it…otherwise what the fuck are we even doing in the same room together.

(beat)

MARI. Why are we, in the same room together, what did you come down here for, to –

GÜERO. México? Oh, I love it down here. In fact, whenever I don't feel like being up there, this is where I'm at.

MARI. Everything is a joke, yes?

GÜERO. Tell me if you're heard this one –

MARI. You look down here for business like business people, but you don't act like business.

GÜERO. Should I wear a suit, carry a briefcase? I have stripper back at my hotel, I'm sure there's some cocaine…around…here…somewhere.

MARI. Why me?

GÜERO. You don't want to know that.

MARI. I asked, didn't I?

GÜERO. You're the Chief of Police, lady. The last thing you want to know is what's going on.

MARI. You're the American, why don't you tell me what's going on.

GÜERO. I'm not going to hurt you.

MARI. That's because you can't. Or won't.

GÜERO. I like you. I do. In fact, I knew that I would. From when I first heard about you. Even from when you contacted the city about volunteering yourself.

MARI. Yea. So you must've heard about what I told to them that day, no? Go on, why don't you recite it back to me. Why don't you wipe that grin off your face, Güero, and recite to me what I said in that room then.

(Music reaches. Both notice.)

GÜERO. The police in this town have no business any longer carrying firearms. A reduction in firearms was a step in the right direction, not just in this jurisdiction, but in every jurisdiction. What is the point of arming more people, when no matter what they do, they will always be out'armed.

(**MARI** *is somewhat taken aback by his accuracy.*)

The only true defense we have is each other. And if we come together as an entity, if all of our families were to become one family, it will be a defense not even the cartels could penetrate. They will kill themselves off with their guns and explosives soon enough, if they didn't have any more of us to draw from. If our children were no longer their one regenerating resource.

(*a moment*)

Sorry, I couldn't get your voice down, you've a softer tone than I.

MARI. And tell me, what is wrong with families watching out for families?

GÜERO. Nothing. Your family is your business.

MARI. Good. So go home then. Leave my –

GÜERO. But it's not your family we're worried about, Mari. These refrigerators, microwaves, alarm whatever –

MARI. It's just music.

GÜERO. When there's a change in the system, Mari, it's my job to find out how it got there? What it looks like. And what it went home to.

MARI. Why did you say that? Went home to. Where is he?

GÜERO. Who.

MARI. *My husband.*

GÜERO. I've nothing to do with your husband.

MARI. You don't have to do this. Whatever it is you're doing.

GÜERO. Neither did you.

MARI. I'll go. Away. You'll never have to –

GÜERO. Hear you again?

MARI. Yes.

GÜERO. If only that were true. If only music was something that could just disappear. Right? That people could forget. But we never do. Music stays with us, doesn't it. Even when I think I've forgotten the most awful song, one day, there it is again. Where did it come from? Why then, why that morning? We may never know the answer to these questions, Mari, about music. It'll be like...one of the wonders of the world. The eighth wonder. Or are we on nine? Anyways. Oh...music. Little insulting that it's so far down the list maybe, but hey, this is far from a perfect world, isn't it.

MARI. You don't have to behave like one of them. You don't have to –

GÜERO. Well, it's a bit late for that. And whoa, speaking of late, we better go.

MARI. Don't you see, those people, *los narcos*, they will do whatever it is that you tell them to. If you tell them no more killing, no more children –

GÜERO. I'm sorry, do you actually know them at all? Because what you're describing would be very out of character.

MARI. They'll do anything you say. Anything.

> (**GÜERO** *opens the station door. We hear cars, gunshots; the music pales in comparison. He motions her to exit first, she does. As she passes him, he stops her*)

GÜERO. Hey. I do. Get it, you know.

MARI. Get what, what is it you get.

GÜERO. Standing here, in this station... I get it why you'd want to, y'know, *do something*. It's like, it almost feels like you could. *(pause)* Anyways.

> (*He motions her to exit, he follows. Lights out.*)

Scene Two

(**EL MORETE** *stands in the* **MARI***'s home. Bound and with a cloth around his head is* **HUSBAND**, *his bag strewn to the side.* **EL MORETE** *texts.*)

EL MORETE. Hey, you got a charger?

HUSBAND. …

EL MORETE. A charger, do you got one.

HUSBAND. For what kind of –

EL MORETE. The best fuckin'kind.

HUSBAND. There's a pocket, on the inside.

(**EL MORETE** *goes through* **HUSBAND***'s bag, pulling a charger.*)

EL MORETE. This one?

HUSBAND. It's the only one there.

(**EL MORETE** *plugs his phone, then pulls a pair of pajama bottoms.*)

EL MORETE. Hey, you actually sleep like this?

HUSBAND. Like what?

EL MORETE. In like, this outfit with the little hearts all over.

HUSBAND. They're pajamas.

(**EL MORETE** *begins searching the house.*)

EL MORETE. You know, I go to like a lot of houses… unexpectedly late at night. And most couples, they sleep naked.

HUSBAND. I don't like to dirty the sheets.

EL MORETE. Hey, tha's what sheets are there for, no? To get all funky an' shit. You don't wanna dirty the sheets, tha's like saying you don't wanna get piss an' shit on your chones.

HUSBAND. It's how I was raised, I guess.

EL MORETE. What, to not-get-the-purpose-of-things?

HUSBAND. To keep things clean.

EL MORETE. Eh, clean is overrated. If you think about like the best times in life, you know, are they like all-the-way organized an' perfectly placed an' shit, or are they the times when you said fuck it an' just let whatever-life-looked-like happen.

HUSBAND. I actually enjoy –

EL MORETE. Yo, the fact that you said "actually enjoy" tells me you don't know what the fuck I'm talking about.

HUSBAND. Look, you're going to do what you're going to do to me, can you just take this thing off my head.

EL MORETE. An' what makes you think I wanna look at your ugly mug.

HUSBAND. You don't wanna look at me when you do it?

EL MORETE. Dime, like, what about a time when you just said FUCK THIS SHIT. Let's talk about that.

HUSBAND. We don't have to talk. You've got me, you've probably got my wife –

EL MORETE. Yo, what kinda man brings up his wife like out the blue like that? Huh? We weren't even talking about ass and you just bring her ass up?

HUSBAND. We have a daughter.

EL MORETE. A daughter?

HUSBAND. Yes.

EL MORETE. Is she like, the invisible kind?

HUSBAND. She's the kind that will need her parents. Even if just only one.

EL MORETE. So tell me something then, for your daughter's sake. When did you say Fuck This Shit for? *(pause)* I'm serious, this a serious question.

HUSBAND. Why're you –

EL MORETE. Answer the fucking question.

HUSBAND. …Me an' Mari used to…

EL MORETE. Yo, there he go with his fucking wife again.

HUSBAND. Hey, you asked me about a time, I'm telling it to you. *(pause)* Me an' Mari used to –

EL MORETE. Used to what, puto, be alive?

HUSBAND. We used to have sex in parking lots –

EL MORETE. See, now tha's how a man brings up his wife for. Go on with that shit, I'm like all ears.

HUSBAND. We would go shopping or wherever, then get all...sweaty. So we'd go back to the car an' hang towels down in front of the windows, so nobody could see. An' just...fuck it.

EL MORETE. Why you stop?

HUSBAND. I dunno. Just...wasn't as...

EL MORETE. How the fuck fucking in a sweaty ass car gets "wasn't as," I don't know, but okay.

HUSBAND. Why did you ask me to talk about that?

> (**EL MORETE** *pulls an unplugged alarm clock, a spurt of his sister's ass spills from it. He looks at it closely, messing with the buttons. A steadiness of his sister's ass comes out of it, regardless what he presses.*)

EL MORETE. So, that parking yard. That junk lot. You two were trying to like...recapture the sweaty magic or what?

HUSBAND. ...

> (**EL MORETE** *puts the alarm clock to* **HUSBAND***'s ear.*)

...We were in the parking lot and she turned the radio and the music started playing and we haven't been able to stop it since.

EL MORETE. Your wife, she was supposed to not make a lotta noise when she took office, at least that's what she tol'people. But *mi familia*, they say that she has made, in fact, a ton of noise.

HUSBAND. She's not, she's not even –

EL MORETE. Your wife run a saw'd off shotgun on my fucking head today. And like family, if she run on shotgun on me, she run a shotgun on my entire line.

HUSBAND. She sawed it off?

EL MORETE. Why does everyone pick up on that shit?! Okay, fine, it wasn't sawed off.

HUSBAND. She would *never* do that, there is no way she would ever…you must have her confused with, or –

EL MORETE. First she play this music when I especially asked her not to, when I especially told how how much I especially hate this fucking song! And *then* she go an' get a fucking shotgun. Oh, an' calling me little and shit. Both of'em.

HUSBAND. Both of who.

EL MORETE. They don't know tho'. They got no idea what I'm capable of. What kinda patience I got up inside me to make this fucking fucked up alarm clock stop playing this estupid fucking song.

> (**EL MORETE** *pulls a machete*)

But they'll see. They'll see me what I do.

> (**EL MORETE** *begins hacking at* **HUSBAND**'s *neck, who lets out a screeching yelp before toppling to the side.* **EL MORETE** *begins sawing through the bone. Blood. When he is done* **EL MORETE** *takes a photo with his phone.*)

> (*On the photo, enter* **GÜERO** *and* **MARI**, *who looks at the room, then eyes* **HUSBAND** *on the floor.*)

> (**MARI** *lets a deafening cry, the music deadens. She goes to* **HUSBAND**, *covering him with their bedsheet. She hums to him. A few moments. She speaks to somebody younger.*)

MARI. *(to* **MIJA***)* "Es okay you cry, Mija. Whatever you wanna do tha's okay. You can even yell as loud as you want, I don't care who hears. You just…"

> (**MARI** *cannot continue, she breaks down. Her crying finds rhythm, she hums to her* **HUSBAND**. *Enter* **DEAD POLICE CHIEF**, **EL MORETE** *startles, backs up.* **DEAD POLICE CHIEF** *looks at the room.*)

DEAD POLICE CHIEF. *(to* **EL MORETE***)* You have no idea the weight of things. Do you.

EL MORETE. ...yo, what the...

> *(****DEAD POLICE CHIEF**** removes his head.* **GÜERO** *flinches, stares.* **EL MORETE** *stumbles back, gun pointed.)*

Hey, whoa! ...like put that shit back on...put that...

DEAD POLICE CHIEF. Do you see, even if all of México were to put down their hands, always there will be little things like you with their little hands up, with their little pistols pointed.

> *(****DEAD POLICE CHIEF**** disarms* **EL MORETE***, grabbing him like a puppet with ease.)*

But lookit now, El Morete, those days are over.

> *(****DEAD POLICE CHIEF**** takes* **EL MORETE** *to* **GÜERO***, who tries to ease the situation, but still listens)*

Lookit him, Americano, this is who answers'to on the other side of your mobile. This is who is *los narcos* with their weapons always drawn, with their voices always so loud. But, do you see what they look like now, do you see how empty?

GÜERO. I do.

DEAD POLICE CHIEF. And tell me, Americano, what about me? Do I look like empty to you now? Do I?

> *(****GÜERO**** shakes his head.)*

You've no idea, do you, how many of us there are out there? Still walking the Earth? Right outside that door. If you had to guess how many, if you had to take a wild fucking stab at our numbers, Americano, what number would you put this little man's knife to?

GÜERO. ...Whose numbers exactly are we –

> *(****DEAD POLICE CHIEF**** drops* **EL MORETE***.)*

DEAD POLICE CHIEF. All who?! ALL WHO!? You Godless motherfucker. ALL OF ME. ALL OF EVERYBODY

LAID OUT ON THOSE CHALK STREETS. ALL OF
EVERY FUCKING HEAD YOU'VE HAD TAKEN. HOW
MANY OF US DO YOU THINK ARE LOOKING BACK
AT YOU, HUH!? HOW MANY!?

GÜERO. ...

DEAD POLICE CHIEF. Well, I'll tell you how many, Americano.
TOO MANY. And we are out there. So, just think to
yourself, here I am just one. Just one of your conquests,
and I've got your complete fucking attention. How do
you think the world will look at you when back outside
there we all are, in the thousands upon thousands, with
our un'dead hands all pointing straight at you.

My guess: You'll shit yourself worse than he just pissed
himself, Americano. And maybe one day you'll be an
empty too. Just like when bullets cross *La Linea*. Oh,
Los Estados Unidos will de' flate. Do you hear me what
I'm tellin'to you, you fuckin'memory.

> (**MARI**'s *humming turns to song. All turn to her.
> Music swells.* **MARI** *illuminates. Enter* **DEAD
> HUSBAND**, *who looks beat, cut up.* **DEAD POLICE
> CHIEF** *goes to him. Both* **EL MORETE** *and* **GÜERO**
> *react, cannot take their eyes off.*)

MARI. Omigod, Love.

DEAD HUSBAND. Always I knew I wouldn't be able to take it
if something happened to you.

MARI. ...

DEAD HUSBAND. But now look at you. Calling me close.
And here I am again. By your side. Just like I should
have always been.

MARI. I'm sorry, I am. For...everything.

DEAD HUSBAND. I should've listened. I should have heard
you what you –

MARI. No, you were right to try to –

> (**DEAD HUSBAND** *kneels, talks to somebody
> younger.*)

DEAD HUSBAND. *(to* **MIJA***)* "Hey Mija, look at who's here? Both your parents here talking."

MARI. *(to* **MIJA***)* "Hi Mija, lookit you, lookit that smile.

DEAD HUSBAND. *(to* **MIJA***)* "We're sorry for all the noise, Mija, we know it must be hard to sleep with all the – "

MARI. *(to* **MIJA***)* "Car backfires."

(*They let* **MIJA** *respond.*)

DEAD HUSBAND. *(to* **MIJA***)* "You're so smart, Mija. And I apology to you. I know you know better than car backfires."

MARI. *(to* **MIJA***)* "He just wanted to protect your little receptors."

(**MARI** *grabs* **MIJA***'s ears playfully.*)

DEAD HUSBAND. *(to* **MIJA***)* "Don't worry though. Look outside the window, Mija, do you know what all that is? That's how bright it'll be now when you walk yourself so safe to that school of yours. An' then pretty soon, Mija, you'll be so smart, that me an' your *Mamá* will haffta ask you what stuff is."

MARI. *(to* **MIJA***)* "You'll haffta explain, Mija, cuz you have it in you to get so smart that we won't even be able to recognize this town where we live. This country. Tha's how different you'll make it with your smart head."

DEAD HUSBAND. *(to* **MIJA***)* "What's that, Mija? Oh, I know, I hear it too. That's how beautiful what your *Mamá* sound like, that's how amazing her voice. And I just cannot wait for you to hear it."

(**DEAD HUSBAND** *stands up taking in the music,* **MARI** *joins him. Music swells.*)

DEAD POLICE CHIEF. If only the world could hear what your family sound like. Me, mine never sound nothing like that. But tha's maybe why I lost my good though, huh?

(**DEAD HUSBAND** *goes to the door, looks out.*)

DEAD HUSBAND. This isn't just us, our family. That out there, that is family.

(**MARI** *and* **DEAD POLICE CHIEF** *joins* **DEAD HUSBAND** *at the door; they all look out.*)

DEAD POLICE CHIEF. We're out there, Mari. Waiting for you. Listening for you. And we are not invisible no more.

DEAD HUSBAND. Look at all of them. Look at how many. You are not alone, Mari.

DEAD POLICE CHIEF. And we will do whatever it is you want, however you tell us to.

MARI. …But, what is it I want?

DEAD HUSBAND. What you always did, to be heard.

(**MARI** *walks to* **GÜERO** *and* **EL MORETE.**)

MARI. And these two. Will they hear me too?

DEAD POLICE CHIEF. They will have to.

DEAD HUSBAND. They already do, Mari. Look at them. If they did not hear all of this that you've created, if hearing you did not –

DEAD POLICE CHIEF. Scare the shit out the them.

DEAD HUSBAND. Thank you. Then they would have gotten rid of you already. But see…

MARI. Tell me, love, tell me what you see.

DEAD HUSBAND. They are the most frightened people here.

MARI. Know what I think?

DEAD POLICE CHIEF. *Dime.*

MARI. They are so frightened, they have no idea we are even standing here.

(**GÜERO** *and* **EL MORETE** *come to from their staring at* **DEAD POLICE CHIEF** *and* **DEAD HUSBAND.**)

GÜERO. Alright, alright.

DEAD HUSBAND. Is it, alright? You don't look aright.

GÜERO. I'll give you that. The fact that you're standing there talking, but at the same time you're sorta laying on the floor over there…bleeding –

DEAD HUSBAND. What about it?

GÜERO. It's...a little...

DEAD HUSBAND. *(to* GÜERO*)* Go on, look for yourself.

(GÜERO *walks to window.*)

DEAD POLICE CHIEF. You Americanos, you see ghosts on all your days, but you never look at them.

(GÜERO *has to hold his hand up as it is so bright.*)

There is nothing little about it, Americano.

On the streets, in your home. But pretty soon, there will be no more homes, there will be just only ghosts. And tell me, Americano, what will you look at then?

(GÜERO *moves away from the window.*)

GÜERO That's uh...quite a view.

(EL MORETE *quietly dials his phone.*)

DEAD POLICE CHIEF. Don't worry, Güero, soon you will be surrounded by so many of us, that my heart cannot even understand it how surrounded. But maybe tha's okay, huh. It ain't my heart that needs to understand it.

(DEAD POLICE CHIEF *takes the phone.*)

(into phone) You can come pick up the little one at *Señora Policia*'s house.

(tosses the phone to the floor)

(to EL MORETE*)* Do you think they'll even come for you.

(to GÜERO*)* Or is he a number already?

(DEAD POLICE CHIEF *walks to the door, he steps out into the music.* DEAD HUSBAND *walks up close to* EL MORETE *and looks at him.*)

DEAD HUSBAND. So, El Morete, would you like to take a look?

(EL MORETE *moves away.*)

MARI. Love.

DEAD HUSBAND. Don't worry, Mari, there is nothing he can do to you now. He hasn't got the voice to even speak at you.

EL MORETE. Yea, you can listen to your "Husband," Mari, or this fucked up music bullshit. But right now, there are real people, with real problems coming your way.

DEAD HUSBAND. To do what? Look outside, what is it you think they can do to her now?

MARI. *(to* **GÜERO***)* Well?

GÜERO. Well, what?

MARI. What can they do to me?

GÜERO. …

EL MORETE. Whatever in fuck they want, Mari. You think they give a fuck about whatever outside whatever door, huh? Es just noise. An' you know what's like louder than fucking noise? Fucking gunshots, fucking automatics being fucking automatic.

So you can stand here with your whatever'the'fuck husband, humming or whatever you do, but in not that long, the only sound that'll be left to heard will be me. My sound. An' that shit'll darken even the brightest motherfucking bright.

> (**EL MORETE** *kneels.*)

"Ain't that right, Mija?"

GÜERO. The hell are you –

EL MORETE. What I always do Güero, exactly what you tell me.

> (*Lights darken outside. Music darkens.* **MARI** *moves to* **EL MORETE***, looking at him with true empathy.*)

(to **MIJA***)* "Hey, es okay, don't be escared.

"Tha's a girl.

"So like, wow, you're big now, what grade are you in anyways? *(pause)* Oh, shit, wha's that you got? You smoke? Hey, tha's okay, when I was your age, I smoke too. It's hard to keep that shit from your parents, huh?

"So tell me, where somebody your age get money for – Oh, what's this?

(EL MORETE holds out a roll of bills to invisible daughter)

"Go on, feel how heavy. *(pause)* What's that? *(pause)* Oh, it does smell nice, don't it. Yea. Hey, know what? You smell nice.

(He kisses MIJA.)

"Believe in this, Mija: you don't need to be escared no more. Cuz you an' me, we belong like to each other, an' no matter whatever happen, you an' me, we're the family now."

(He stands. Lights and music resume, but affected.)

DEAD HUSBAND. You don't listen to him, Mari. She'll be okay, our Mija will grow up to be –

EL MORETE. The fuck she will.

(EL MORETE takes back his gun and exits.)

GÜERO. ...I just want you to know, Mari, that this whole... everything, can be cleaner than it is. And whatever I can do to make it a nicer exchange, I will.

MARI. A nicer exchange?

GÜERO. A nicer exchange.

MARI. This is no exchange. This is as one'way as life gets. And there is nothing close to nice even about it.

GÜERO. Nice'er. I did say er. Oh, also, I'm thinking we should go.

MARI. Go where?

GÜERO. Y'see, at the end of the day, you are...

DEAD HUSBAND. Don't listen to him. He has no idea what you are.

GÜERO. Well, she's alive. But in a very short time I'm thinking a whole crew of men with guns are gonna pull up here and shoot her repeatedly.

MARI. So, what, you're helping me now?

DEAD HUSBAND. He can't help you. Outside, Mari, outside is the only help you need

GÜERO. I can take her with me.

MARI. What?

DEAD HUSBAND. Take her where.

(**GÜERO** *points north.*)

MARI. What do you mean, what are you –

GÜERO. I'm talking about what if you could be on television, Mari?

DEAD HUSBAND. He's desperate, Mari, he has no –

GÜERO. As the bravest woman this side of México. You'll be in the papers; online and off. News anchors will want to interview you about you. About what happened to your husband. How did this twenty-two-year-old you with a family of her own decide to…well, we know the story.

MARI. And I'll get to go with you, across…

GÜERO. Look, I've got no shot of quieting whatever all this is in this country, but I've got a pretty good shot of making you famous in mine. And well, my country is, if nothing else, somewhat louder than yours.

DEAD HUSBAND. Did you hear him, he can't quiet you, Mari. Nobody can. Not him, not *los narcos*, not *los soldados*, not –

MARI. And what do you get?

GÜERO. Mari, your "husband's" right, I can't have all this… noise. In the business sense of it. And while I know business is entirely the opposite of what you care about, if you don't come with me, your entire line of family, will be…just like him.

Which, I'm sorry, might sound like music to you now, but we're talking Grotesquely. Fucking Torturously.

DEAD HUSBAND. Los narcos will pull up here to where we live, Mari, to where our daughter will one day wake, and they will not be able to do anything. They will put their hands up to stop the bright, and drop their weapons so they can stop up their ears.

GÜERO. What they can't do today, Mari, they can do on another day. You know this. But if you come with me, if you bring your family along too, nobody will ever be able to reach you, because your story will be...heroic. And shit, do we Americanos love us some heroics.

MARI. And if I go with you, Americano, if my family comes along. What happens to *la música*? Will it be heroic too?

GÜERO. Look, going with me is the humane thing to do here –

DEAD HUSBAND. For which country? Ours or yours?

GÜERO. You want there to be less dead, less bodies.

MARI. But is that what you want?

GÜERO. Yea, alright, fine. I'm a selfish prick, nine outta ten women will agree. But that one, that one woman out of ten will tell you, Mari, that your parents will want you to come with me, your sister and her family will want you to live, no matter what the cost. They'll say to you that one day you *could* have a daughter –

DEAD HUSBAND. She will have one.

GÜERO. Okay. And that daughter will thank you for all her life, for letting her have a life. And her kids will too. And their's after.

MARI. Es a simple question, Americano, what happens to *la música* if I go with you?

DEAD HUSBAND. And imagine what can happen to *la música*, if you doesn't go with him.

(**GÜERO** *pulls his mobile.*)

GÜERO. Look, I've made my offer. It's your life to take or let go of. Just say the word. And if you don't say the word...well...then good luck to you, you best be on your way. And me on mine.

(*They stare. A moment. He dials, lights darken over him. Music bursts through, it crosses countries and expands borders.* **MARI** *and* **HUSBAND** *look at each other as they listen in awe at the vibrations of the music. White out.*)

CLOSING

(**EL MORETE** *looks up at the sky as it brightens, as the music soars.*)

(*Several hundred ghosts appear. He pulls his gun and aims it in all directions. Lights drown over him.*)

(*Inside the home is messy; drawers are opened, clothes strewn about. It is vacated and looks exactly like the sort of house you would see a decapitated man laying in a pool of blood. From outside, the sounds of tires crushing onto gravel are heard. Headlights flash in the window. Several car doors open and shut. The music swells, drowning out the sounds of footsteps on gravel moving closer and the clocking of automatic weapons.*)

(*When the stage has hit to black, we hear men's voices entering the home, shouting through it. Fragments of phrases such as: "¡¿Donde están?!" and "¡No están aqui!" can be heard. The music grows in strength over the voices, silencing them. Deafening in beauty before spilling over into the sort of serenity that just does not exist anymore.*)

(*curtain*)

End of Play